I0530514

The Lost

Keeper

A Short Thriller by

Wiley McLaughlin

The Lost Keeper

Lighthouse Series

Lighthouse Series
First Print Edition: August 2017
Volume: 1

All images for book are copyright: 123RF stock.

ISBN: 978-0-692-93293-3

To my mother Gloria and her two sisters Anona and Lula Ethel. The best "Three Amigos" that ever lived.

Photo: 1993 personal collection of Cynthia Williams.

The Stephenson Sisters

Table of Contents

Acknowledgments

My first acknowledgment must go to my spouse Linda. She was supportive through the whole process.

My old friends Janet Carpenter and Liz Mathews were huge contributors to this book. Janet was instrumental in editing and helping me write this book. Liz was always helpful locating information and ready to lend an ear anytime.

Special recognition goes to my cousin Lois Ann Stephenson. Her enthusiasm and excitement gave me the inspiration to create a historical piece of fantasy.

Chapter 1

Campfire

May, Friday the 8th, 1857: weather is fair, light winds, clear sky with a full moon tonight. We are camping within sight of the Powers dock and general store. Live Oak Point is bustling with activity this evening. It's past sunset and becoming dark quickly. I can see in the distance several silhouettes of ships and boats anchored near shore. Oil lamps and lanterns are coming to life, like twinkling stars on the water. Mother calls my name, "George, bring your brothers and come to the fire. Your father is ready to tell that story." Richard and John Lee are running while holding hands, and younger John Lee is dragging a stick through the wet, hard-packed, fine sand. All three of us are barefoot and in a race to the campfire. In the dry sand near shore, we all get settled around the small blazing fire. My sisters, Mary, Priscilla, and Amelia, already have their places, as we all are excitedly awaiting father's story.

Mother, Caroline Stephenson, throws another arm full of collected beach wood on the fire. The fresh wood causes the fire to blaze, and embers float up around our mother. In the glow of the campfire, you can see our father, James. Father resembles a Greek war hero with his blue eyes, shoulder-length blond hair, clean-shaven face, and athletic suntanned physique. He has a jovial personality, and is always telling me "George, remember, treat each day like a holiday and every meal like a banquet." I love to hear his war stories, like how Father, Grandfather and Uncle John helped General Sam Houston at the Battle of San Jacinto. But, tonight he has promised a new ghost story just for us kids.

Father begins. "OK, children let me tell you the story of the Lost Keeper. It all happened at a nearby shoreline much like the one around this campfire. Several ships that passed by the Aransas Lighthouse reported strange sightings. The legendary Capitan Jose Gaspar tells this story of the frightful and unexplained, which plagued the shores around that beacon of light".

The Lost Keeper

Chapter 2

Captain Jose Gaspar and the "Sherman"

In the emerald green water sits a yellow and white, two mast Caribbean schooner, gently rocking back and forth. Across the stern, the name "Sherman" is smartly spelled out in black letters. The "Sherman," crew of six, seventy-two foot long and twenty foot wide with its ten-ton cargo of salt is in route for St. Mary's. She has been on the Gulf three days from the port of Tampico, Mexico.

As the wind whistles through the rigging, Capitan Jose Gaspar is standing at rear quarterdeck. He is a tall man with many scars on his face; the most notable is under his left lower jaw. He has scraggly, dark, shoulder length hair, along with a clipped mustache and beard. Gaspar wears a naval-type dark blue coat with gold buttons, gold cords and crimson cuffs. His hat is large, round and dark, with dazzling decorations. On his left ring finger is a large silver lion's head, which shows his status as leader. His weapons include a long knife and a flintlock pistol. Gaspar won his gun in a duel against a Caribbean pirate. Gaspar is confident, experienced, eloquent, and persuasive. He considers himself a gentleman of the seas and could act politely if he wished.

But this is not a time for polite behavior, as tensions are high. Captain Gaspar, with clenched fists on hips, grimly looks over his crew. He addresses the crew in a booming mandate, "Look sharp and listen to my every word! We are crossing the bar in a half hour's time. With this wind and the tide against us, there is no room for mistakes. We're light today, but still drafting one fathom. Stay on deck! No man below! Be ready! Quartermaster Smith, take the wheel."

As Gaspar considers what is to come, he knows that crossing the shallow sand bars is never easy. Will the current overpower the wind? Will the men react to needs of the ship? Will the gap in the channel be wide enough this day?

While searching for the mouth of the inlet, Gaspar finds the new lighthouse on the horizon. Pleasant memories of the Danish lighthouse keeper, Anton Anders, bring a smile to his face. Anton, small in stature, fair skinned, blue eyed, with a bright smile, is always holding his tobacco pipe. With so many stories shared, the one that gives Gaspar the shivers is the Island Mustang tale.

The Lost Keeper

The Island Mustang is a sinister animal and is said to lurk close to shore. This beast is found in a maze of dunes. Accounts tell that it can appear as a gleaming white stallion. Some reports claim it can change to a bright silver or gray. When people get close enough, they will realize this is no ordinary horse; his mouth is full of razor-edged teeth, which can rip you to shreds. Its beauty often fools children, and they all want to ride him. It doesn't matter how many wish to climb on his back, for the horse's back can grow to any length to accommodate every child that wants to ride. When all the children are seated and comfortable, the Island Mustang will gallop into the water, never to return to shore.

With eyes closed, Captain Jose Gaspar can almost hear the distant hiss of foam bubbles dying on the beach.

The Lost Keeper

The Lost Keeper

Chapter 3

Crossing the Aransas Bar

Captain Jose Gaspar is standing on the quarterdeck, with eyes studying the shore and reading the wind. He seems to be waiting for a sign. A sailor calls out from the bow, "Breakers on the second sand bar, Sir!" Captain Gaspar retakes the wheel and commands, "Quartermaster, have your men ready. Set her at full sails. We're going down wind and against the tide!" Smith screams, "Men, at your stations, make full and fast! Gybing on the port, have jib sheets ready... NOW!" Springing into action, the crew rushes to their stations, aloft and on deck. Like the beat and rhythm of the breaking waves, the men begin unfurling the sails and trimming the jibs. All hands are getting the "Sherman" ready for her test with the inlet.

Gaspar is steering the "Sherman" due east. His plan is to sail across the wind and abruptly turn to the port side at just the right moment. Sufficient speed is critical to prevent capsizing. In eight minutes, Mr. Smith is able to deliver the speed. As Gaspar calculates the turn, they arrive at the second sand bar in the breakers. Gaspar presses his lips tightly together as he assesses their progress. He only needs fifty more yards.

At last it is time. Capitan Gaspar orders, "Mr. Smith, Gybe-ho, hard to port; let's don't get caught in the irons." The men make half main sail and reverse the aft and bow jibs. With swells at five feet, the breaker comes over the port side. Gaspar's clothes are drenched. The "Sherman" neatly heels over twenty degrees. At this moment, their fate is in the hands of the crew, and they deliver. They bare-up-round in just enough time to outrun the next breaker. With the roar of the surf now at a distance, the crew's concerns wane. Gaspar relaxes for the last turn, "Mr. Smith, half on the mains, half on the jibs; were headed for the dock across from the lighthouse".

After the turn the "Sherman" sits nearly motionless. The outgoing tide is almost slack, but not just yet.

Chapter 4

Lighthouse Keepers Death

Captain Jose Gaspar notices more activity than normal along the water's edge. On the south shore lays the sleepy community of St. Joe's Island, about thirty wooden houses. Several women and children are walking along the water's edge; they seem to be looking for something. Northwest of the channel is Mustang Island. No boats are docked at the Mercer station. This is an unusual sight, for on most days at least three pilots' boats are moored at her dock.

Gaspar gets an eerie feeling in his belly and goose bumps along his arms. Gaspar commands, "Crew, scour the waters and have gaff hooks in hand. All ahead slow and steady." A cry from the bow, "Capitan, you need to come see this! In the water is a sail." As Caption Gaspar gets to the front of the boat, he sees a sunken canvas on the water. Nearby is an overturned, small, red-bottomed sloop, which slips deeper into the channel. Gaspar wonders what had happened to the steersman, and whose boat this is?

As the "Sherman" had struggled with the second sand bar, Anton Anders had steered his vessel through the rough waters of the channel. An angry sea took offense and attacked him. Everything was immediately lost. He became entangled with the main sheet. His trap was set; he was like bait on a hook.

The Sea whispered, "You'll drown before the water lets you in." Anton's stronghold on earth was instantly a past perception. The small red sloop unshackled his trap and released him from all sorrows. Like a buoy, he was suspended as he waited for this endless rest.

The surge of a thousand waves propelled his body toward fathomless depths, to the rushing, triumphant, outgoing tide. With this last embrace, the Sea whispered, "You'll drown before the water lets you in." Anton Anders is lost to the sea.

The "Sherman" slips in starboard along the north end of the Aransas dock. Before the men can moor and make secure, Capitan Club appears at the dock. Club and Gaspar exchange greetings, "How on earth is the ugliest Caribbean pirate able to acquire such a fine crew?" Gaspar responds "A promise of gold, and an opportunity to incarcerate the scally-wag Captain Club. Happy to see you, my friend. What is going on here?" Club says, "Well, we are all looking for the lighthouse keeper, Anton

Anders. The dock men here report that they saw Capitan Anders stumbling and getting wrapped in his main sheet and then his boat suddenly capsized." Gaspar explains, " Yes, just as we came in, we found a small red boat engulfed by the outgoing tide about two hundred yards from here." Both men peer silently in the direction of the tragedy.

The hours turn into days as the community searches for Anton. There is even talk of exploding dynamite in the channel with the hopes of raising the body.

The Lost Keeper

Chapter 5

The Harbor Island Banshee

Captain Club recruits the most respected and experienced seamen from the Aransas area to help with finding Anton's body. Anton's widow, Agnes Anders, is still in denial of her husband's death. She is consumed with the thought that he is merely lost and only needs to be found.

Death has brought overwhelming sorrow to Agnes' life. Just three months prior to the loss of her husband, Agnes lost their eight-year-old son, Harry. He was aboard a small boat in the channel while returning from an outing with his friends, Mark Mercer and Sam Brundrett. The three were out collecting oysters near the shell bank, as they had done many times before. But this time Harry slipped, hit his head, fell overboard, and drowned.

Capitan Jose Gaspar and the crew of the "Sherman" continue with their delivery of salt to St. Mary's. On their return trip, he brings Agnes' sister,

Elizabeth, from Corpus Christi. Elizabeth has come to help Agnes through this troubled time. Elizabeth finds that her sister is overrun with anxiety and still anticipates Anton's return. During daylight she finds Agnes, atop the lighthouse, searching the nearby shores. At night, Agnes walks the long dock at the lighthouse and continues along the shore, with a lantern in hand, calling Anton's name. Elizabeth sees that the poor woman has become exhausted, incoherent, and out of her mind with grief. It troubles her that no amount of sisterly companionship or sympathy is quieting Agnes's pained spirit.

The most mysterious and frightening event happened on the next full moon. Elizabeth is standing on the lighthouse pier. Agnes runs past Elizabeth, swiftly down the steps, and onto the beach. It is past twilight, and the tower is beginning to push the bright beam from its crown. The giant, radiant moon has come out of its slumber and just now has risen fully from the sea. At that magical moment, as the first flash of light from the lighthouse beacon illuminates Agnes on the beach, a surreal transformation begins to take place. The bright light surrounding Agnes becomes a greenish-blue glowing mass, much like a jellyfish drifting in the sea, and seems to consume her body. Several bright spherical balls of light zoom above her like departing fireflies. Her spirit becomes momentarily visible as it decays from the inside out and her soul slithers away. All that seems to be left is a transparent flowing aberration of an old lady holding a glowing lantern. The Harbor Island Banshee is born.

The current lighthouse keeper claims that on several occasions during broad daylight he has heard footsteps on the lighthouse staircase, but finds no one around when he investigates. Passing ships have seen an old woman at the top of the tower with a spyglass to her eye as if searching the shores. On full moon nights, the townsfolk of St. Joe's Island watch carefully from across the channel as an old lady holding a glowing lantern walks the lighthouse grounds and beaches. Sometimes the distant weeping of a broken-hearted woman can be heard. If the wind is calm, and the waters are quiet, one can hear the Banshee's wailing "Anton…Anton."

The Lost Keeper

The Lost Keeper

About The Author

Wiley McLaughlin lives south of Bandera on a small family ranch. He is a native Texan, born and raised in Corpus Christi. In the course of his historical research, Wiley McLaughlin discovered that several of his ancestors played significant roles in the history of Texas. After a career as a geologist, Wiley returned to Corpus Christi where he worked at a refinery for nineteen years. Now in retirement he drives a school bus. He indulges himself, with writing about his ancestors and the Texas Coastal Bend history.

The Lost Keeper

Also by
Wiley McLaughlin

Lighthouse Series

Coming soon

- Kindle version The Lost Keeper
- Pirate Jose Gaspar
- Island Mustang
- Harbor Island Banshee
- The Grace Darling Story
- The Frank and Mindy Love Story

The Lost Keeper